DUNCAN'S
TREE HOUSE

For
Anna,
Milly
and
Johnnie

First published in Great Britain by
HarperCollins Publishers Ltd in 1992
First published in Picture Lions in 1992
7 9 10 8
Picture Lions is an imprint of the Children's Division,
part of HarperCollins Publishers Ltd,
77-85 Fulham Palace Road, Hammersmith, London W6 8JB.
Text and illustrations copyright © Amanda Vesey 1992
With special thanks to Camilla for her drawing.

The author/illustrator asserts the moral right to be
identified as the author/illustrator of the work.
ISBN: 0 00 664239 X

DUNCAN'S TREE HOUSE

ᐧ AMANDA VESEY ᐧ

PictureLions
An Imprint of HarperCollins*Publishers*

On his birthday, Duncan's parents gave him a tree house. Duncan's father was a builder. He had made the tree house in his workshop and he had fixed it to the tree the night before Duncan's birthday, when Duncan was asleep. It was a complete surprise to Duncan.

Inside the tree house was a camp bed and a rug and a
table and a chair and a shelf with cups and plates on it.
There was a bookcase and a tin box for keeping things in.
The window had real glass in it, and opened and shut.

Duncan leaned out of the window and waved to his parents in the garden below.

"Thank you!" yelled Duncan.

"I'll put up a sign so that everyone will know whose house it is," said Duncan.

He carved DUNCAN'S TREE HOUSE with his penknife on a piece of wood, and painted it.

Then he nailed it to the hand rail outside his front door.

Duncan spent most of his time in the tree house.

He pinned posters on the walls.

He put toys in the tin box and books in the bookcase.

He played with his monsters from a Lost Planet game, his space shuttle and his remote-control moon buggy.

He didn't have to tidy them away.

Sometimes his mother gave him a picnic so that he could stay in the tree house all day.

He could play his radio as loud as he liked and there was no one to tell him to turn the music down...

...but if he wanted a nice restful silence there was no one to disturb him, either.

Sometimes Duncan
watched the birds
and squirrels through
his father's binoculars.
When he didn't
know the names of the
birds, he looked them
up in his bird book.

Sometimes he drew pictures of the view from the tree.
He could watch a neighbour hanging out the washing,
the boats on the river and the tractors in the fields.

One day, Duncan had an idea.

"I want to spend a night in the tree house," said Duncan.

His parents weren't sure.

"Are you sure that's a good idea, Duncan?" asked his father.

"Are you sure you won't be lonely all by yourself?" asked his mother.

Duncan was sure.

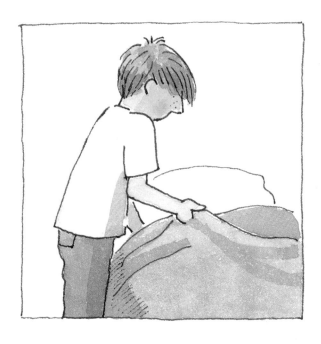

Duncan put extra blankets on the camp bed.

He borrowed a big torch from his father and checked the batteries in his pocket torch.

He packed up a midnight feast in case he got hungry in the night.

He couldn't wait for bedtime.

"I'm off now," said Duncan, after supper.
His mother gave him a flask of cocoa and a hot-water bottle.

"Take Buster with you," said his mother.
"Buster is big and brave. You'll feel safer
with him."

Buster was fat and unused to ladders. Duncan coaxed
and wheedled and pushed and pulled. In the end he had
to heave him up, step by step.

Duncan put on his pyjamas and his dressing gown. There wasn't any running water at the tree house so he didn't have to wash, or clean his teeth.
He sat outside his front door and read a book until it grew dark.

"Time for bed," said Duncan.

He switched on the torch. It was a powerful torch, but the light didn't reach into the corners. Tall black shadows sprang and danced across the room.

"I expect we'll feel cosier in bed," said Duncan.

The bed faced the window. There were no curtains; outside was inky black.

"Suppose something horrible climbs up the ladder and peers through the window," thought Duncan. "Something terrible with yellow eyes and great pointed teeth – "

Crash! Something thumped against the window pane.

Duncan put his head under the bedclothes.

It was only a moth, attracted by the light.

When he fell asleep, Duncan had a nightmare about wolves.
"Yowl! Wail! Yelp!" howled the wolves, as they chased
him through a forest.

Duncan woke up, but the howling didn't stop.
It was Buster who was howling. He was
scratching at the door. Buster wanted to go out.

Getting a fat dog up a ladder in daylight is one thing.
Getting a fat dog down a ladder in the dark and carrying
a torch is another.

When they reached the ground Buster waddled off into
the darkness.

"Come back, Buster!" cried Duncan.

Come back! Come back! Duncan's voice echoed through
the trees, as he stumbled through the undergrowth. Black
clouds scudded across the moon. The night was alive with
hootings and screechings and rustlings. A great white owl
swooped out of the shadows. Branches clawed at Duncan;
brambles tore his clothes.

Something was moving through the bushes. A grunting Something, a huge heavily breathing Something, snapping twigs as it came nearer. And nearer...

Duncan fled back towards the tree house. The Something followed close behind him.

Crash! Duncan missed his footing in the darkness and landed face downwards in a bramble patch, dropping his torch.

"Help!" cried Duncan as the Something landed on top of him.

It was Buster.

*   *   *   *

The tree house felt welcoming and safe. Duncan sat up in bed and ate a bar of chocolate.

"You don't deserve any chocolate," Duncan told Buster. But he gave him a piece all the same.

Crack! The tree house was lit by a great flash of lightning. Boom! Boom! Thunder rolled overhead. Then came the steady hiss of rain.

The rain became a deluge. It lashed against the window and drummed on the roof. The tree house shook and shuddered with every thunder clap.

Buster was afraid of thunderstorms. He clung to Duncan while the storm raged over the tree house.

"This is the worst night of my entire life," said Duncan.

When Duncan woke, the sun was streaming through the window. The birds in the tree were singing and bickering and calling to each other.

"Wake up!" said Duncan, "it's a beautiful morning."

Duncan and Buster sat outside the front door and shared the midnight feast.

Duncan watched a fisherman on the river bank, and the swallows swooping over the water. A breeze rustled the leaves of the tree. There was a smell of damp earth, and everything looked fresh and sparkling after the rain.

"Breakfast time, Duncan!"
  It was his mother, calling from the foot of the ladder.
"Did you have a good night in your tree house?"

"Brilliant," said Duncan.